Small Fur Is Getting Bigger

by IRINA KORSCHUNOW
with pictures by REINHARD MICHL

translated from the German
by JAMES SKOFIELD

HARPER & ROW, PUBLISHERS

Small Fur Is Getting Bigger
Copyright © 1986 by Verlag Nagel & Kirnche AG, Zurich
Translation copyright © 1990 by Harper & Row, Publishers, Inc.
Printed in the U.S.A. All rights reserved.
1 2 3 4 5 6 7 8 9 10
First American Edition, 1990

Library of Congress Cataloging-in-Publication Data
Korschunow, Irina.
[Kleiner Pelz will grösser werden. English]
Small Fur is getting bigger / by Irina Korschunow ; translated
from the German by James Skofield ; illustrated by Reinhard Michl.
    p.   cm.
Translation of: Kleiner Pelz will grösser werden.
    Summary: Small Fur has trouble standing up to his gruff uncle and
relating to his friend Curly Fur, until an incident in the swamp
convinces him of his self-reliance.
    ISBN 0-06-023289-7 : $. — ISBN 0-06-023290-0 (lib. bdg.) :
$
    [1. Self-reliance—Fiction. 2. Uncles—Fiction.] I. Michl,
Reinhard, ill. II. Title.
PZ7.K8376Sp 1990   89-26747
[E]—dc20   CIP
                                                         AC

Small Fur Is Getting Bigger

*S*mall Fur sat next to his mother on the stove bench and listened as she told him stories. The winter wind howled outside the house and rattled the shutters. But it was snug and warm in the kitchen, and it smelled of baked apples, honey, and nuts. The logs crackled and snapped in the fire.

"It's good to be sitting inside," said Mother. "Winter is very nice by a warm stove."

Small Fur shook his head.

"No," he said. "Summer's much nicer. I wish it were summer."

Small Fur was tired of winter. The long winter. It was cold and dark. When Small Fur

went outdoors, he sank to his stomach in the snow. He couldn't play in the forest or go see his friend Curly Fur. It wasn't much fun to build pinecone houses or draw pictures of squirrels and rabbits alone.

Small Fur was bored. The apples and nuts didn't taste good anymore, and he knew by heart all the stories his mother told about gurgle-ghosts, fog-witches, and tree-spirits. Still the snow kept coming down. It snowed and snowed and wouldn't stop.

"It will soon be spring," said Mother, stroking him. "Soon you'll be able to run in the forest again."

"Good," said Small Fur, and was happy.

"In the spring Uncle Ned will come and fix everything the winter has broken."

"Uncle Ned!" Small Fur was so upset he swallowed a nut whole. "Why does he have to come? I don't like him. He grumbles all day, just like Aunt Grouch."

Mother stopped stroking him.

"Uncle Ned is nice. Last year he fixed our roof and painted the house. He even built you a swing!"

"Stupid swing," Small Fur said, and went over to the window. He breathed a hole in the frost on the windowpane and looked out into the darkness. The wind was chasing snow flurries. It roared and howled and wailed. It sounded just like the gurgle-ghosts out in the swamp.

"Uncle Ned should visit the gurgle-ghosts instead," thought Small Fur.

Spring finally came. The snow melted and disappeared. The sun coaxed leaves from the buds and flowers from the ground. The forest grew green and bright once more.

Small Fur forgot winter. Together, he and Curly Fur patched the holes in the tree house. They built a new hideout of moss and branches and sod. They played ball and caught fish and chased squirrels, just like the year before.

But now this year they were bigger and braver. They ran deeper into the forest than before—all the way to shaggy Trulla's hut. They even dared to go as far as the swamp, the squishy, muddy swamp where the gurgle-ghosts lived.

"Small Fur," his mother had said again and again, "if the gurgle-ghosts ever catch you, they'll keep you forever."

"I know," said Small Fur. He didn't let on how close to the swamp he and Curly Fur had been.

The days grew longer and warmer. When the lilies-of-the-valley were in bloom, Small Fur and Curly Fur decided to build a raft.

"It's easy," said Small Fur. "All we have to do is tie a few branches together. Then we'll travel all the way down the river."

"All the way to the end of the forest?" asked Curly Fur.

"Even farther," said Small Fur. "We'll go around the world."

But it wasn't so easy to build a raft. First they had to drag the thick branches down to the river, and that took a long time. Then Curly Fur held the branches while Small Fur tried to tie them together with willow bark. But the branches kept slipping out of place.

"We're not strong enough," said Curly Fur sadly.

"Yes, but we still want a raft," said Small Fur, and so they began all over again. They sweated, they got their fingers bloody and their fur full of splinters. And still the raft was far from finished.

Small Fur threw the willow bark down and said, "Let's try again next week. We'll be bigger and stronger next week."

"Do you think so?" asked Curly Fur.

"I am sure."

Suddenly they heard far-off voices. They were howling and roaring. Gurgle-ghosts!

"Let's go!" said Small Fur. "We might see a gurgle-ghost."

They went to the swamp and sat under the willows and waited. It was quiet, quiet as only a swamp can be after the gurgle-ghosts have stopped singing.

"I'm going home," said Curly Fur.

Small Fur tossed a couple of pebbles into the swamp.

"Are gurgle-ghosts really black?" he asked.

"Black and muddy," said Curly Fur, "and if one comes, I'll run home."

"Me, too," said Small Fur, "but I still want to know what they look like."

"What if they catch you?"

"Not me." Small Fur threw another stone into the swamp. "Gurgle-ghosts are much too stupid."

"How do you know that?" asked Curly Fur.

"Because they live in this slime," said Small Fur. "Would you live here?"

Curly Fur shook his head.

"You see," said Small Fur, "they're stupid. That's why we can tease them a little."

He stepped closer to the swamp's edge and called:

> Gurgle-ghosts, burgle-ghosts,
> Hurgle-turgle-murgle-ghosts,

"Cut it out," said Curly Fur.

But Small Fur went on:

> Feeble-ghosts, beetle-ghosts,
> Creepy heebie-jeebie-ghosts,
> Mixer-ghosts, fixer-ghosts ...

Something stirred in the swamp.

Bubbles rose to the surface and burst. The reeds rustled.

"Gurgle-ghosts!" screamed Curly Fur, and ran.

Small Fur ran too. But he stopped and hid behind the willows and looked back.

A figure was sitting in the swamp—a small black figure. It was covered all over with slime, from its long hair all the way down to its feet.

"Hello, Small Fur," called the figure, and waved to him.

Small Fur didn't know what to do. Stay? Run away?

"Better run away," he thought. But he stood still and waited.

"Hello, Small Fur," called the figure again. "I'm a gurgle-girl."

Gurgle-girl? His mother had never told him about gurgle-girls.

"Come closer," called the gurgle-girl. "Then we can play together."

Small Fur was confused. Gurgle-ghosts had no faces, his mother had said. No eyes, no nose, no mouth. That's why they couldn't speak—only howl and wail. But his mother had never seen a *real* gurgle-ghost.

"Come closer," called the gurgle-girl again.

Small Fur stepped back.

"You come here," he mumbled.

"How can I? I can't come out of the swamp."

"And I don't want to get in it."

"Too bad." The gurgle-girl moved a little closer to the edge. "It's so nice here, and I know lots of great games."

Small Fur craned his neck. He looked for the gurgle-girl's face. All he could see was slimy black hair. He took a step forward, and suddenly the ground under him felt soft and wet.

"You have to be careful with gurgle-ghosts," thought Small Fur, and quickly stepped back.

The gurgle-girl laughed. "Are you afraid of me, Small Fur? I won't hurt you."

"How come you know my name?" asked Small Fur.

"I've known you for a long time," said the gurgle-girl. "That's why I'll let you look in my magic mirror. Would you like to?"

Small Fur hesitated.

"You can see everything that's going on in the forest in it."

"There's no such mirror," said Small Fur.

"And I have a ball. A very special ball. Made out of silver and gold."

"Silver and gold?" Small Fur had never seen a ball made out of silver and gold. He didn't even know there was such a thing.

"Would you like to see it?" asked the gurgle-girl.

"All right. Where is it?" Small Fur leaned forward. The mud squished under his feet. It squished and squelched and gurgled and suddenly he found himself up to his ankles in water.

"Come closer," cooed the gurgle-girl, "and I will give it to you."

Small Fur sprang back.

"No! I'm not stupid enough to go into the swamp!" he yelled, and he ran home. The gurgle-ghosts weren't going to get him!

When Small Fur got home, his mother was at the edge of the forest, gathering wood for the stove. Small Fur thought gathering wood was boring, and he usually hid in the bushes when he was supposed to help.

But now he gathered a whole basketful and even carried it into the woodshed.

"What's wrong with you today?" asked his mother.

"Nothing," mumbled Small Fur.

He wanted to tell her about the gurgle-girl, but he knew his mother would scold him.

"Maybe tonight," he thought. He took a piece of cake from the kitchen and sat down on the bench by the door.

The sun shone. Two blackbirds hopped through the grass, fighting over a worm. Small Fur threw them some cake crumbs. They dropped the worm and pecked at the crumbs, their tails bobbing.

Small Fur leaned against the warm wall of the house. He raised his arms and stretched. He was happy he was sitting in the sun and not in the wet, cold swamp.

Suddenly he heard footsteps. Uncle Ned appeared from around the corner with his backpack and his tool kit.

"Good day, Small Fur," he bellowed. "Good day. I am here. Let me look at you, Small Fur. Well, you've grown, and how! A proper Coal Fur. Yes, yes, time flies. Haven't you got better things to do than feed birds? The proper food for them is worms! Shoo, shoo, get along, you garbage grabbers!"

The blackbirds flew away into the forest, and Mother came running out of the house.

"If it isn't Uncle Ned!" she cried. "What a surprise! Did you have a good trip?"

"Good trip!" Uncle Ned shook his head. "What a silly question. It was hot and dusty."

"Yes, of course, Uncle Ned." Mother took Uncle Ned's backpack. "Come inside and take a little rest," she said.

But that didn't sit too well with Uncle Ned.

"Did I come here to rest?" he bellowed. "When there's so much to do? There's the fence, and the window shutters hanging crooked. And I'm supposed to rest? Take a rest in the sun, never get your day's work done. Coal Fur, you can carry my tool kit. Now step lively, lad."

Uncle Ned and Mother went into the house. Small Fur trailed behind them carrying the heavy tool kit.

Uncle Ned sat in the kitchen and ate cake. He slurped and swallowed one piece after another until the cake plate was empty. Then he folded his hands over his belly and said, "No Fur was ever hurt by food and drink. Keep your belly full, and your work's a jewel. Isn't that right, Coal Fur?"

"That's *not* my name!" yelled Small Fur.

Uncle Ned paid no attention to him. He

opened his tool kit and said, "First, we'll build a new fence."

"A new fence?" cried Mother. "Can't you just repair the old one?"

Uncle Ned said that would be a waste of time. "And I don't waste my time. I'll measure everything tonight and begin tomorrow. Coal Fur can help me. He'll finally learn how to handle a hammer and saw."

Small Fur crept close to Mother and she stroked him.

"Next year, Uncle Ned," said Mother. "This year he still needs time to play."

"Play?" Uncle Ned thundered. "No good will come of playing and stroking. They'll never make a strong, able Fur out of him. Isn't that what you want him to be?"

"Well, I guess you're right, Uncle Ned," Mother said.

"Of course I'm right." Uncle Ned nodded happily. "Let me see your arms, Coal Fur. Do you have good muscles?"

"No," said Small Fur.

"Don't you do push-ups?"

"No," said Small Fur.

"And handstands?"

"No! No! No!" yelled Small Fur.

Uncle Ned shook his head. "When I was your age, I was the strongest young Fur far and wide. I could run on my hands almost as fast as on my feet. All the other Fur children were scared of me. Wouldn't you like to be like that?"

Small Fur was about to say no when Uncle Ned grabbed him by the legs and lifted him, head-over-heels, into the air.

"Ten-shun!" he cried. "On your hands! Stand on your hands, Coal Fur. Thataboy! That's the way to do a handstand!"

"No!" screamed Small Fur, and fell flat on the floor. He lay there until Mother helped him back onto his feet.

"Did you hurt yourself?" she asked.

Uncle Ned laughed. "You're a sissy, Coal Fur. That'll have to change." He clapped him on the shoulder. "Never fear, we'll make a strong, able Fur out of you yet."

That night when Small Fur went to bed, the moon was shining into his room. Small Fur had always found that pretty before, the moon and stars so near over his bed. But tonight he didn't even look at the night sky.

"I don't want to be Coal Fur," he said to his mother.

"That *is* your name," she said. "And Uncle Ned is right—you should learn some things. Help him with the fence."

"I don't know how," said Small Fur.

Mother stroked him. "Uncle Ned will show you how."

"I don't want to learn anything from him," said Small Fur. He hid his head under the quilt.

The next morning Small Fur was awakened by the blackbirds. He sprang out of bed, pulled his pants on, and was about to run to Curly Fur's house when Uncle Ned stopped him at the front door. Small Fur tried to slip by, but Uncle Ned held him fast.

"Good morning, Coal Fur," he boomed. "Do you always sleep so late? Get cracking! Nimble hands at break of day whisk our troubles right away. Go eat your honey bread and then we'll start."

Small Fur sat down at the kitchen table. He ate one piece of honey bread after another.

"Aren't you full yet?" asked Mother.

"No," said Small Fur, and kept on chewing

very slowly, until Uncle Ned came into the kitchen to get him.

And then they started. They went into the forest to look for slender tree trunks. They piled them into a wagon and brought them home. Uncle Ned sawed them into slats. Then he ripped off the old fence slats and nailed on the new ones.

Small Fur tried to help, but he did everything wrong. The slats were too heavy for him, the axe and the saw too big. He didn't know how to hold the hammer properly. And Uncle Ned bellowed at everything he did—and bellowed and bellowed.

"Get with it, Coal Fur! Pay attention! Are your fingers made of mashed potatoes? Not

so slow, not so slanted, look over here, don't be lazy, work harder."

"I am, I *am*," muttered Small Fur, holding back tears.

"No you're *not!*" Uncle Ned hit a slat with the hammer so hard the board cracked. "I knew it all along—you're a sissy. A new wonder of the world, a Fur with two left hands!"

After that, Small Fur stopped trying and just stood around with his hands in his pockets.

"You're not Small Fur, you're not Coal Fur, you're *Lazy* Fur!" roared Uncle Ned.

Small Fur was miserable.

Mother tried to comfort him. "Uncle Ned doesn't mean any harm. And we're getting such a nice, new fence."

She stroked him. But what good was being stroked when she wasn't making sweet honey pudding for him?

"Pudding's unhealthy," Uncle Ned had pronounced on his first day. "Sticky stuff gives you bad teeth. Vegetables and roots are what a Fur needs. Chew upon a root tonight, keep your chompers shiny-bright. Look at *my* teeth! Pretty good, huh?" He opened his mouth wide.

"You almost never see such good teeth, Uncle Ned," Mother said.

From then on, all Small Fur got to eat was lettuce leaves and thick root soup.

After three days, the fence was finally finished.

"Now it will have to be painted," said Uncle Ned.

"Whatever for?" asked Mother. "It looks pretty just the way it is."

But Uncle Ned said, "Only a green fence is a clean fence! Take the brush, Coal Fur. Painting's not difficult. You can certainly do it. Always go from the top to the bottom, and no drips, understand?"

Small Fur crouched in front of the fence. He dipped the brush in the green paint and began. It went pretty well. It really wasn't hard. It was even fun.

"I can do this," he thought. "Such a nice green. I think I'm a very good painter."

Mother thought so, too. She stroked him and whispered, "Soon we'll have honey pudding again."

Then came Uncle Ned. He looked at the fence. He looked at Mother and Small Fur and shook his head.

"It's too thick here, too thin there, and spattered all over with paint drips. Scrape the mess off, Coal Fur. The second time will be better. Even if a Fur is small, he can master something tall."

33

"No!" yelled Small Fur.

"Now don't be obstinate," said Mother. "Uncle Ned is right; anything new has to be learned."

She reached out to Small Fur, but Small Fur didn't want to be stroked.

"Yucky fence!" he yelled, and hurled the brush away. "Disgusting, dirty, yucky fence!"

"Pick up that brush right now, Coal Fur!" bellowed Uncle Ned.

"No!" screamed Small Fur. He stamped up and down on the brush. "No, no, no!"

"Do as Uncle Ned says," cried Mother.

And so Small Fur ran away. He left Mother and Uncle Ned standing there and ran to Curly Fur's house.

Curly Fur was sitting in his backyard building a tower out of pebbles and moss.

"Want to help?" asked Curly Fur.

"No," said Small Fur. "That's dumb."

Curly Fur got up. "Want to go to the tree house?"

"Dumb tree house," said Small Fur.

"How about our raft?"

"That's dumb too," said Small Fur.

"You're dumb yourself," said Curly Fur.

He got his ball and his fishing net and ran to the stream. Small Fur gave the tower a kick, then trudged after Curly Fur. He didn't feel like playing ball. Or catching fish. And he never wanted to see the raft again.

"What do you want to do?" asked Curly Fur.

"Nothing," said Small Fur. He lay down

among the tall ferns by the stream. He crossed his arms behind his head and stared up at the sky. It was a beautiful summer sky, all blue and white, with cloud ships sailing by. But Small Fur didn't see the white clouds or the sun. He saw only the fence and Uncle Ned and his mother. His mother saying, "Uncle Ned is right."

Curly Fur was blowing on a blade of grass. "Show me how, Small Fur. You can do it so well," he said.

"Leave me alone," said Small Fur, and pushed Curly Fur onto his back. Suddenly they heard footsteps. Curly Fur raised his head but ducked right back down.

"Trulla!" he whispered.

Small Fur peered through the ferns. Trulla came shuffling along out of the thicket with her wood pack strapped to her back. Gray hair fell over her face. Her dress and her shawl were also gray. Shaggy, gray Trulla. She stopped by the ferns and with her crooked staff dug out a root. She sniffed the root and muttered something to herself.

Small Fur hardly dared to breathe. He had never been so close to Trulla. Once he had snuck around her hut, but very quietly, so she wouldn't know.

Trulla had been living in the forest for the last two summers. No one knew who she was or where she came from. "When you see Trulla, run," Mother had said. "Who knows what she does back there in the clearing." Small Fur scrunched himself down among the ferns and didn't move.

"She's gone now," said Curly Fur. "Were you scared, too?"

Small Fur was about to nod yes when he thought of Uncle Ned and said, "Naaah. Not of Trulla."

"Well, I was," said Curly Fur.

"Sissy," said Small Fur.

Curly Fur got mad. "Who's a sissy? My mother thinks Trulla's a fog-witch!"

"Don't make me laugh," said Small Fur. "She lives in a house, you know."

"And she kidnaps Fur children in the night."

"That's not true," said Small Fur.

"Is so," said Curly Fur.

"Is not."

"Is too," yelled Curly Fur.

"You're stupid," yelled Small Fur.

Curly Fur jumped up. "And you're mean and nasty. A real Stinky Fur. I don't want to be your friend anymore." He grabbed his ball and ran home.

"Don't go, Curly Fur. I didn't mean it," Small Fur wanted to say. But he couldn't get the words out. And now it was too late.

Small Fur fell back into the ferns. He lay there until the sun disappeared behind the trees. Then he stood up and walked deeper into the woods. He didn't see the flowers, or the birds, or the squirrels. He also didn't pay attention to where he was going. And so he came to the swamp.

Evening mist lay over the black pond. No blade of grass stirred, no mosquito buzzed. At the edge of the slime sat the gurgle-girl.

Small Fur was scared. His heart thumped loudly. His hands grew cold and clammy. He wanted to run away, but just didn't know *where.*

"I've been waiting for you, Small Fur," said the gurgle-girl. "Are you *still* afraid of me?"

Small Fur shook his head. He didn't want to be scared. He wanted to show Uncle Ned how

brave he was. Uncle Ned and Mother and Curly Fur—all of them.

"How did you know I was coming?" he asked.

"I saw it," said the gurgle-girl, and raised her hand. "What do you think I have here?"

"A dirty black thing," said Small Fur.

The gurgle-girl laughed.

"It's my magic mirror. You know, it shows me everything that's going on in the forest."

"I don't believe that," said Small Fur.

"You don't need to," said the gurgle-girl. "I see what I see, that's enough."

Small Fur was silent. "What do you see, then?" he asked.

"I won't tell."

"Do you see Curly Fur? Is he still mad at me?"

The gurgle-girl did not answer. Small Fur stepped nearer to the swamp. His feet got wet, but he didn't notice it.

"And is Uncle Ned finished with the fence yet?"

"Look in the mirror if you want to know," said the gurgle-girl.

Small Fur reached out and felt the ground squoosh with dampness under him. "Beware of the gurgle-ghosts," his mother had warned. But he wasn't thinking of her just then.

"Here," said the gurgle-girl. "You may have my mirror. Because you're such a nice Fur."

"Really?" asked Small Fur.

"The nicest Fur I know," said the gurgle-girl.

Small Fur leaned forward and reached for the mirror. Suddenly the gurgle-girl grabbed his arm and pulled him into the swamp.

"No!" screamed Small Fur. He tried to get free, but the gurgle-girl held on tight. They pushed and pulled in a tug-of-war. Small Fur felt the ground grow softer and more slippery. He was up to his knees in the slime.

The gurgle-girl laughed. She didn't sound friendly anymore. Her laughter sounded as horrible as the singing of all gurgle-ghosts.

"Help!" screamed Small Fur.

"Stop screaming," said the gurgle-girl. "I'm taking you with me to our black home. It's wet, and dark, and cool down there. It's much nicer than up here in the sun."

Small Fur kept on screaming. He screamed for his mother, and for Curly Fur, and even for Uncle Ned.

But it was Trulla who came. Gray, stooped, and shaggy, she shuffled out of the thicket and raised her crooked staff.

"Begone, gurgle-girl! Leave the Fur alone. Begone!"

44

The gurgle-girl shrieked furiously.

"The Fur is in the swamp. Whoever is in the swamp is ours!"

Trulla swung her staff through the air, and the gurgle-girl howled loudly. She spat out mud and slime. But when Trulla raised her staff again, the gurgle-girl let go of Small Fur and sank back into the swamp.

"Just you wait, Fur, we'll get you yet," she screamed as she sank into the swamp.

Trulla kneeled down and pushed her staff toward Small Fur.

"Hold on tight," she said. "I'll try to pull you out, but you'll have to help me."

"But how?" wailed Small Fur.

"Don't howl," said Trulla. "Think of some-

45

thing nice instead. Something you'd lose if the gurgle-ghosts got you."

"Will that help?" asked Small Fur.

Trulla nodded. Small Fur thought about home. He thought about the kitchen table and about his bed and about the bench by the front door. He thought about his mother and how she sat beside him and stroked him every night. He thought about Curly Fur and the river and the world they wanted to explore together. He thought about sweet honey pudding and the tree house and the stream with the fish. While he was thinking of all this, Trulla was pulling on the staff. She pulled and Small Fur pushed, his feet planted against a root. Finally he scrambled out.

"I did it," he gasped, and fell into the dry moss.

Trulla threw down her staff. "I've sprained my arm. That's what happens when a stupid Fur takes up with a gurgle-ghost."

Small Fur started to cry.

"Now, don't wail," said Trulla. "Come here and calm down."

Small Fur sat down next to Trulla. The moss was still warm from the sun. The leaves over him rattled in the wind. Two squirrels romped through the branches.

"Anyone who's been as lucky as you should be happy," said Trulla.

"I am happy," said Small Fur, and moved closer to Trulla. She still looked scary. Her face was as wrinkled as a last year's leaf. Her gray hair hung down to her nose and a big black tooth stuck out of her mouth. But Small Fur wasn't afraid of her anymore.

"Does your arm hurt?" he asked.

Trulla nodded.

"I'll help you back to your hut," said Small Fur. "I can carry your wood pack."

"What's your name, anyway?" asked Trulla.

"Small Fur," said Small Fur. "Well, Coal Fur, really. But I like Small Fur better."

"Small Fur?" Trulla shook her head. "My wood pack is much too heavy for a small Fur."

Small Fur looked at the wood pack. It was filled with wood.

"I can pull it. Like a sled."

"Let's go, then," said Trulla.

It was a long way to the hut, and the wood pack was heavy. Trulla took some pieces out, but it didn't help much. Small Fur had to rest again and again.

Finally they reached the hut. It stood in a clearing at the edge of the forest. Long ago a storm had knocked over the old oaks, beeches, and birch trees; now new trees had grown, thick and dark.

"Come inside, Small Fur," said Trulla.

It was cold and damp in the hut. Small Fur set down the wood pack next to the stove. He was about to sit down on a bench when Trulla asked him, "Do you know how to start a fire?"

Small Fur shook his head.

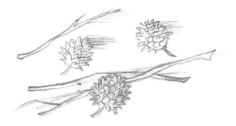

"My arm is numb and it hurts," said Trulla, "and I'm hungry and cold."

"Me too," said Small Fur. "What do you want me to do?"

"Open the stove lid," said Trulla, "and blow on the coals."

Small Fur blew on the hot ashes until the coals were red and small flames sprang up.

"Throw pinecones and dry branches on the fire," said Trulla, "and thick logs on top of them."

Small Fur did as she said. The fire began to burn and the stove top grew hot.

"You did that well," said Trulla. "Now warm the soup."

The soup was green; as green as grass, with leaves and blossoms in it. "Mixed herb soup," said Trulla. "Be careful — don't burn yourself."

Small Fur placed the pan on the stove. He stirred until the soup steamed. Then he filled two bowls and carried them to the table.

It had grown warm in the hut. The fire in the stove crackled; the soup smelled like the forest. Small Fur forgot how unhappy he was.

"Mixed herb soup tastes good," he said.

"I like it too," said Trulla. "My mother made it often when I was as small as you."

"As me?" Small Fur asked, surprised.

Trulla laughed. "Do you think I've always been old and bent? I used to make herb soup for my children, too."

Small Fur looked at her shaggy hair and the black tooth.

"Where are your children?"

"Gone."

"All gone?"

"They left," said Trulla. "Many Furs leave home when they grow up."

"Now you're all alone?" asked Small Fur.

"Yes," said Trulla. Small Fur would have liked to stroke her, but he didn't know if Trulla would like that.

Trulla fetched a lantern and lit it. In the flickering light she looked even odder than before. Small Fur stirred his soup, and he counted the leaves floating on top.

"Is it true that you can do magic, Trulla?" he asked.

"Magic? No, I have no magic."

"Too bad," said Small Fur.

"Why?"

"Because then you could do magic so that I wouldn't be a sissy or a Lazy Fur any longer and I'd do everything right."

"A sissy?" asked Trulla, and shook her shaggy head. "*And* a Lazy Fur? Who said such nonsense?"

"Uncle Ned. And he said I'd never be a big, proper Fur."

"Your Uncle Ned said that?" Trulla laughed. "He must be a very dim-witted uncle."

"Don't know," said Small Fur.

"Don't know, don't know. Didn't you escape from the swamp?"

"That was because you helped me."

"Anyone who escapes from the swamp is no sissy," said Trulla. "And you carried my wood pack, and made a fire and warmed the soup. Would a Lazy Fur do that?"

"Don't know." Small Fur put his spoon

down. He had been so happy. Now he was sad again.

"It's too bad you don't know magic, Trulla," he said.

Trulla thought awhile. She sat there silently and did not make a move.

Small Fur was silent too.

Finally Trulla stood up. She got a jar of honey and put it on the table.

"Eat some honey, Small Fur. My honey will make you strong."

Small Fur tried the honey.

"It tastes just like the honey at home," he said.

"Perhaps," said Trulla. "Perhaps not. And perhaps I can do a little magic. But you'll have to help me."

"How?" asked Small Fur.

"Stand up," said Trulla.

Small Fur stood up.

"Take a spoonful of honey."

Small Fur did so.

"Now look at me," said Trulla. "Look at my black tooth and repeat twelve times, *I'm no sissy and no Lazy Fur.*"

"This is magic?" asked Small Fur.

"Do as I say," ordered Trulla, "but don't stumble over your words!"

Small Fur did what Trulla told him. He stared at her black tooth and repeated—"I'm no sissy and no Lazy Fur, I'm no sissy and no Lazy Fur, I'm no sissy and no Lazy Fur..."

The tooth began to grow. It grew bigger and bigger. It grew so big that Small Fur saw only

the tooth and not Trulla's face. His arms and legs itched. His back and his stomach started itching too. But Small Fur kept repeating, "I'm no sissy and no Lazy Fur," twelve times in a row and he didn't stumble over a single word, not once.

When he finished, the itching stopped. The tooth shrank back. It grew smaller and smaller until it was once again a tooth in Trulla's mouth.

"The magic worked," she said.

"You think so?" asked Small Fur.

"Absolutely," said Trulla. "You'll soon see. Now we'll go to sleep."

Small Fur went to the window. It had gotten dark in the forest. Through the black trees he could see the night sky.

"I have to go home," he said, "or my mother will think the gurgle-ghosts got me."

"All alone through the dark?" asked Trulla. "Aren't you afraid?"

"Yes," said Small Fur. He'd never been out in the forest so late. He didn't know if he'd find the right path, and he was scared of the fog-witches and tree-spirits.

Trulla gave him her lantern. "That'll help against fog-witches and other creepy, crawly creatures. Will you bring it right back?"

"Tomorrow," said Small Fur. "I'll bring Curly Fur too. He'll be surprised when he sees you."

"Why?" asked Trulla.

Small Fur didn't answer.

"Tell me why," said Trulla.

Small Fur shook his head and went to the door. But then he stopped and turned back.

"Because Curly Fur thinks you're a fog-witch."

"He thinks so, does he?" asked Trulla. "What if I really am a fog-witch?"

"No!" cried Small Fur. He ran to Trulla and laid his head against her patchwork skirt.

"Good luck, Coal Fur," Trulla said, and stroked him gently.

Holding the lantern high, Small Fur stumbled through the black forest. "Hoo-hoo, hoo-hoo," called the owls. Tree-spirits grabbed at his legs from the underbrush. Fog-witches lurked with their gray nets in the clearings.

"Come with us," they whispered. "Come with us."

When Small Fur shone his lantern at them, they melted into the darkness. But they always came back, again and again. And all the while the gurgle-ghosts were singing their songs in the swamp.

Small Fur ran through the forest. He didn't know where he was. "Any minute, they'll grab me," he thought.

Suddenly the voices faded. Small Fur saw his house, and his mother at the front door.

"Small Fur!" she cried. "My Small Fur! Where have you been? I was so worried."

She hugged him close and did not stop stroking him. Small Fur forgot the tree-spirits and fog-witches and gurgle-ghosts. He was home!

"I'll make you some sweet honey pudding," said Mother.

Uncle Ned was sitting in the kitchen.

"Runaway!" he bellowed. "Where were you hiding?"

Mother put the pot on the stove.

"Hush, Uncle Ned," she said. "Can't you see how tired he is? He needs something to eat."

"But why honey pudding?" Uncle Ned bellowed so loudly the plates clattered. "Honey-pudding and bed-so-soft never made a Fur child tough! Bread and water is what a runaway deserves."

Small Fur looked at Mother. "I knew it," he thought. "I should have stayed with Trulla."

Mother took a deep breath. "Now hold your tongue, Uncle Ned!" she said angrily. "Leave my Small Fur alone! That's enough!"

Uncle Ned was so surprised that he couldn't even bellow.

"So that's enough, is it?" he grumbled. "Suppose I left? Who'd paint the fence?"

"Nobody," said Mother. "We don't need a green fence. In fact, we don't need a fence at all."

Uncle Ned sprang to his feet.

"That does it. Help a needy Fur get by, and you're doomed to curse and cry. Well, you can just take care of your garbage yourself!"

"Uncle Ned!" Mother called after him.

But Small Fur said, "Now we'll be happy again."

He ate his pudding and went to bed. Mother stroked him and he told her about Trulla and the swamp and about the fog-witches and tree-spirits. But he said nothing about the gurgle-girl. He didn't want to worry Mother.

"I hope Uncle Ned doesn't change his mind," thought Small Fur as he fell asleep.

When he woke next morning, Uncle Ned was gone.

That afternoon, Small Fur got Trulla's lantern and went to see Curly Fur.

Curly Fur was in the front yard. He was bouncing his ball against the wall and pretended he didn't see Small Fur.

"Hi, Curly Fur," said Small Fur.

Curly Fur didn't answer.

"Want to come with me?" asked Small Fur.

Curly Fur let his ball bounce.

"You're not my friend anymore."

"That's not true," said Small Fur.

"You said I was stupid."

"C'mon," said Small Fur, "you're not stupid. Please come with me."

"Where are you going?"

"To Trulla's," said Small Fur. "She's not a fog-witch—you'll see. We'll return the lantern to her and then we'll build our raft."

"We won't finish it," said Curly Fur.

"Maybe we will," said Small Fur. "Please come with me."

So Curly Fur tossed his ball away, and he and Small Fur ran into the forest.

"Don't run so fast, Small Fur!" called Curly Fur.

Small Fur stopped.

"From now on, don't call me that. That's not my name."

"What is it then?" asked Curly Fur.

"Coal Fur," said Small Fur. "I like Coal Fur much better."

Irina Korschunow, a well-known German author of books for children, has had a number of her books translated into English, including THE FOUNDLING FOX, ADAM DRAWS HIMSELF A DRAGON, and SMALL FUR, all published by Harper & Row. In recognition of her writing, she was nominated for the Hans Christian Andersen Award in 1986. Ms. Korschunow lives in Grafath, West Germany, near Munich.

Reinhard Michl is well known as an illustrator in Europe. He was born in Lower Bavaria and studied at the Academy of Pictorial Arts in Munich.

James Skofield translated THE FOUNDLING FOX and ADAM DRAWS HIMSELF A DRAGON by Irina Korschunow and is the author of three books for children: NIGHTDANCES, SNOW COUNTRY, and ALL WET! ALL WET!